Starfish

Anne Eton

This paperback is also available as an ebook at most online ebook retailers.

Copyright 2013 Beginnings Press

ISBN-13: 978-1-62602-029-0

ISBN-10: 1626020299

Jill's waiting by the fountain. Just like she said she would be.

She sees me and smiles. Her hand touches her short blonde hair and I wonder if, under all that armor of cool, she's just as nervous as I am.

I say hi, try to crack a joke. She says something about my outfit. How she didn't think I owned clothes like this.

Looking down, I consider my midriff—baring red blouse, black jeans, black studded belt and Cruella heels. It's all stuff I picked up in thrift stores over the years. I always shop thrift. Usually I purchase my regular conservative clothes. But the sexy blouse was a quarter, jeans were a buck, I think the shoes came as a two-pairs-for-one buy but I'm not sure. I can't resist a good deal. I told myself at the time that I was assembling a Halloween costume. I would go to a party as Jill.

Only that never happened, along with so many

other things. Throwing the clothes on today had been a last-second decision. I had wondered if Jill would get the joke.

She certainly looks amused. Dressed same as ever. Tight white shirt exposing her flat tummy, black hip huggers, black sneakers. But there's a light in her eyes. She smiles at me, and I forget what I was going to say.

She walks, I follow. I wonder if our local hangout will be jammed with parents and their kids, celebrating today's graduation. We trot over the quad, where custodians are setting up the folding chairs in precise, orderly rows. Power tools hum as bored burly guys assemble a stage, panel by panel.

The bar is indeed packed but Jill, as usual, finds a way. Soon the two of us have improbably found stools at the bar. I order a vodka martini, something I've only had once before. Beer is my go-to, whenever I'm not with Brad, anyway—he disapproves of drinking and who can blame him, I should, too—but right now there's no time to lose. Jill and I only have a few hours. I need some liquid courage, fast, if I'm going to go through with this.

The martini arrives. I try not to gulp it. Jill sips a Blue Moon, her usual. We discuss moving-out stuff: rental trucks, boxes, dollies. I keep glancing at the clock on the wall. Relax, Jill says. It's going to be okay. I tell her I know, but deep down I don't know.

My phone rings. Brad. I answer it and shout over the bar noise that I can't talk right now. He asks me where I am, and I tell him, but I add that I'm with my parents. He says okay, and that he will see me at graduation. We hang up.

If I had told him I was with Jill, maybe he would have invited himself to join us. Fifty-fifty, I think. Lately he has acted, not hostile exactly, but cold whenever Jill has been around. It's as if he senses a competitor, another suitor. Or maybe he's just plain jealous. He knows nothing about The Offer, though, so I guess he just has good intuition.

Way back, when Jill originally asked me to say nothing to Brad about The Offer, I had rolled my eyes. Brad and I at the time had been dating for less than a week. Not telling him about The Offer had seemed like a waste of a good joke.

Jill and I had laughed about The Offer ever since freshman year. It annoyed me that Brad could not share in the mirth. But Jill had made me promise.

Now I'm glad she did. Brad knows nothing about Jill's sexuality and things are so, so much easier that way. His intolerance in that regard is one of the few things I don't love about him, and it would break my heart if he came between Jill and me. Jill's friendship has been the one constant of my up-and-down college journey. I feel close to her in a way that I fear Brad will never understand. But he doesn't need to understand, and that's okay.

I order a second martini and down the hatch it goes. Jill cracks that she doesn't want to have to carry me. I kid that she might have to. It's like old times, us teasing and laughing. I try not to think about leaving tomorrow…

I'm not thinking about it. And I can tell Jill's refusing to think about it either. She small talks: her new job, the studio apartment in Manhattan that she has rented sight unseen, the possibility that she may buy a bike and brave New York's city streets. Working on Wall Street is boring enough, she says. A hair-raising commute twice a day may keep life interesting.

I'm feeling the alcohol now. Good. A light, easy buzz lifts my brain. Everything seems funny—the jostling crowd around us, the posters on the wall, Jill's starfish earrings. I've never seen her wear them before.

I bought them for her during sophomore year, when she and Deborah and Bonnie and Elizabeth and the rest of us were in Fort Lauderdale on spring break. The earrings were in a costume jewelry bin inside a tourist trap gift shop. My gift was a joke, of course. I had earlier begun telling Jill that she was a starfish, and I was a clam. She kept applying relentless pressure, trying to get me. No matter how many times I had told her to forget about The Offer, she had never given up. The starfish earrings had made her laugh, like she laughed about everything.

I suddenly remember something. *If I wear them, will you accept The Offer?* Jill had asked then.

The shiny stainless-steel earrings look pretty under the bar's track lights. I reach and touch a glittering starfish, sliding my finger over Jill's ear. Jill gets a funny look on her face. It's an expression I've never seen before, and for a moment I almost run out, run away, leave her with the check and everything else, all the memories, the friendship, us. Because I'm terrified of the possibility that in the next few hours the *us* will stop, and in its place there will just be a *me* and *her*. That might happen, anyway, since she is going to the Big Apple and I'm going to be teaching English in Botswana with Brad. Out of sight, out of mind.

Alcohol-brave, I go ahead and ask her: is this going to change our friendship?

She smiles. She takes my hand. That will never, ever change, she says. I nod. I believe her.

My hammering heart slows and my face transforms into a sunny smile.

Our drinks are empty. You ready? she asks, touching my knee. It's a light touch, just her fingertips, a playful touch like so many she has given me over the years, but this time it shoots electricity up my legs.

I pay for my drinks, she pays for her beer. We slide off our barstools, jostled by the hovering frat boy seniors desperate for a seat and one last get-wasted-hurrah before graduation in a few hours. Jill leads me out into the sunshine.

She turns back toward campus. What? Oh, yeah. The conference center. As I walk behind her, stumbling in my heels, my alcohol-fogged brain struggles to remember the conversation we had had less than an hour ago.

I had called asking where she was going to sit. What do you mean, she had said. After a short chat about potential shaded areas on the quad and saving ourselves from the traditional graduation-day sunburn, the words left my mouth. Out of nowhere.

I wish I taken you up on The Offer.

(A timely pause as she weighs if I'm kidding. She decides not, thus:)

It's not too late.

(I laugh. She speaks again.)

It's not too late.

(Her tone deflates my giggling. Calm. Sure of herself. Very Jill. She keeps talking.)

Why don't we go to the conference center. We don't have time for a hotel. My roommate's here, and I'm guessing your roommate is there, too. Right?

Right.

So let's do it.

(An eternity passes. Finally, I reply:)

I need a drink first.

Meet me at the fountain. We'll hit the tavern and then we'll go. Okay?

Okay.

See you in five.

Okay, I had said. I look at the tree limbs swaying above us in the breeze as we pass through the heart of the place I have spent the last four years of my life.

Okay, I had said. Just *okay*. No *aw Jill*. No *yeah in your dreams*. No evasions or brush-offs or snappy comebacks. Not today. Not on this, the last day we will see each other for a long time.

Inside the conference center, a few older men in suits wander around. They seem befuddled. Probably visiting professors, wondering what all the commotion is about on the quad and forgetting it's graduation day.

Jill approaches the reception desk. I halfway hope they have no rooms, and am halfway terrified they don't.

They do—someone canceled their reservation. Jill pulls out a credit card.

I can pay half, I say.

She gives me her trademark grin. Points to me, says: Peace Corps salary. Points to herself: Wall Street salary.

I laugh. She pays. If the receptionist wonders why two college girls are renting a six-hundred-dollar-a-night room at the campus conference center on graduation day, she doesn't show it. She's probably seen more interesting stuff than this.

We rise up the elevator in silence. I touch Jill's hand; her fingers caress mine. The doors open and she walks out into the hall. My hand releases, and she doesn't hold on; I hurry out after her before the doors close again.

Room 662. I feel an incredible wave of relief that we are not in 666, an indicator that I would be going to hell for sure. Then I remember: no hotel has room 666, or room 13 for that matter. So if I am looking for a sign that my betrayal of Brad is going to send me to eternal damnation, I'm not going to find it in such a soap-opera overwritten way.

Jill walks past the bed, pulls the curtains closed. She glances back over her shoulder.

I'm still on the threshold.

We stare at each other.

Finally, I walk in and close the door.

For a moment, I wonder if all Jill really wanted to do was watch HBO. The TV remote's in her hand. Stations flip endlessly before she finds what she wants: smooth jazz. A screen saver glides around the television screen and soft saxophone music fills the room.

You romantic you, I say. Only it doesn't come out right. My voice is high and catches on the last word. I wonder if Jill will feel sorry for me and call the whole thing off. *That's all right, Ellie, we don't have to do this. Why don't we just lie on the bed, order some champagne, and relax?* I see us laughing on the bed, fluted glasses in hand, reliving all the funny stories of the past four years.

Jill sees my nervousness all right, but her

reaction isn't exactly what I was expecting. She begins popping the buttons on my blouse, one by one. Her eyes are on her work and you would think from her calm expression she was just helping a friend disrobe in a cabana at the beach.

It hits me how determined, how ruthless, she is. The straight-A student. Ceaseless letters and phone calls to investment banks, asking for an internship. No wasted time. Guess that applies in this area of her life, too. Jill has always known exactly what she wanted, which I suppose is partly why she's always fascinated me. I came to college with a vague idea of doing some sort of philanthropy work. Beyond that, I didn't know. I guess I still don't.

My shirt's off. Jill reaches for the belt. I don't want to be undressed like a child so I beat her to it, opening the buckle carefully, watching the sharp spikes in the leather. The damn belt stabbed me once when I was rearranging my closet and I don't want it to happen again. Stepping out of my heels, I unzip my jeans before stepping out of them also. After a split-second I scoot my panties off and beat her to that, too, because somehow I want to own the responsibility.

But it doesn't matter, because I freeze up anyway. So Jill takes the lead. Turning my shoulders gently, she faces me away from her. My head bows. I'm embarrassed, scared, pick an adjective. I've never felt so unsexy in my life.

But Jill's hands communicate with my body, rubbing my hunched shoulders. It's okay, the hands tell me. It's okay.

Gradually, I feel some tension drain off. Now I just feel foolish. Jill's soft lips kiss the back of my neck, as if to say: *giving up so soon? You hippies always were quitters. Ha ha, kidding.* Kiss, kiss...

Her hands brush my hair over my shoulders and my curls settle on my chest. I feel my bra unhooked, the first time another person has ever done that. Looking down, I watch the cups pull away from my dark locks as Jill slides the straps down my shoulders. It's a huge effort for me not to cover myself with my arms.

Her hands leave my shoulders. I hear her undressing. I just wait—head bowed, facing away, thinking about freshman year.

Our very first day together, Jill and I had agreed that some smart-ass must have assigned us together as roommates. Why else would a crunchy liberal do-gooder be paired with someone who actually declared in her admission essay that she wanted to be a millionaire by 23? We had laughed about it, then gone to our very first meal in the cafeteria.

I feel her hands again. Gentle pressure. She's turning me. I comply, passive. Facing her, I can't yet look her in the eye. I stare down, goggle-eyed at the naked gym-toned body that I have seen a million times before. Freshman year, anyway, the last time we roomed together. But it looks like not much has changed. Why would it have?

This is the interval when I expect the speech. *Don't worry Ellie. We can take this slow. It'll be beautiful, you'll see.*

Nope.

She takes my hand, tugs. I look up. She's smiling. Walking backward, she leads me into the bathroom.

I can't quite process her joke, something about room-servicing a camera for Girls Gone Wild. My mind is not registering the words. I just stand on the cold tile. Jill pivots and bends into the tub to turn on the water.

I consider, in an abstract way, her butt. It's round and firm with a perfect little V indentation at the top where the cheeks meet. Why can't I have that butt? I know what Jill would say: you can, if you work for it. But my college gym membership was wasted on me. I think I went once, to stare at the treadmills. Perhaps consequently, my own butt has been growing over these past four years. This month I finally bit the bullet and bought new underwear and jeans, since who knows how many thrift stores there may be in rural Africa. Has Brad made comments about The Incredible Expanding Ass? Probably, but I tune him out. I tune out a lot of what he says.

Hot water sprays from the showerhead. A warm steamy mist settles over my skin. Jill lifts the bathmat from the edge of the tub. Watching her lay it on the tiles with a perfect flip of her wrists, you would think she does this every day. Her boobs wobble with the movement, a saucy shake.

I try not to wonder if this is Jill's standard seduction technique: lead a nervous first-timer into the shower for some loosening up, then repair to the bed. How many times have I seen her hook up with some girl at a house party, some girl who more often than not had had no idea that she might on some occasion try going gay for a day. Or a night. I would watch Jill lead them upstairs, downstairs, or out through the exit. I asked her once what her secret was; she said that the straightforward approach always worked best. I like you, you like me, homosexuality.

The humming exhaust fan overhead can't keep up with the steam. It's filling the bathroom and beading on my skin, running down in drops. Jill smiles at me through the fog and embraces, snuggling in close. Here we go. I close my eyes. We're standing next to the tub. I worry about falling on the tub if I pass out. I'm feeling pretty lightheaded. As Jill begins kissing my neck softly, so softly, my brain keeps thinking about the best decision to make in the short second or two before I faint. Fall toward the towel bar and try to grab it on the way down. At least maybe I'll slow my body when it hits the tile...

Jill's kisses advance toward my Adam's apple. I

tilt my chin high. Opening my eyes, I look up at that stupid ventilation fan embedded inside the light fixture. You would think for this kind of money a hotel would splurge on something that could actually suck steam out of a bathroom. Oh my goodness. I gasp, hard.

Jill stands up again after having given my pubic hair a lick. What the hell? It's hard to hold my thoughts together. But Jill just snuggles in again, kissing and nibbling the other side of my neck. Her hand cups my breast, as soft a touch as I have ever felt in my life.

I put my hands on her. They settle on her hips, like we are dancing.

I say ow and flinch as something sharp jabs my clavicle. Jill notices and touches her ear. The starfish earrings are duly removed and placed on the sink counter.

I smile as she returns for the embrace, opening my arms to her this time. We kiss. Just a light brushing of lips that connect so slightly it almost doesn't happen at all. Tingles explode over my skin.

We stand by the side of the tub forever as Jill's light kisses wander over my neck and shoulders. Her hands begin to caress the Incredible Expanding Ass. I catch myself, chastising my brain for thinking that way: you're pretty, everybody says so, and neither you nor your butt are fat. If Brad wants to comment every time you eat a bite of cheese or chocolate, you can just start making remarks about his disappearing hairline.

Jill kisses up the tip of my chin to my cheek, a slow dreamy diagonal line bypassing my mouth. I turn my head and push my lips onto hers. They open. Our tongues touch, a tentative hello.

She pulls away gently and I have to let go. Checking the water temperature, she bends over again, adjusting the faucet. My fingertips slide a big goofy happy line up and down her back, matching my big goofy happy smile.

She enters the tub. I take her hand and also step daintily over the edge, feeling the warm water wash away the steam and sweat on my body. Our faces close, she grins in response to the big goofy happy smile. Kisses my cheek. Then she moves close again, kissing my neck once more. I don't think I could ever get tired of this.

We're not snuggling, not that close. It's like she's teasing me, daring me to crush my body into hers. The tip of her tongue slides down my neck aaaalllllllllll the way to my breast. Her lips cover the peak. I never knew a touch so soft could make me so crazy. As her fingers touch my pubic hair, I wonder what took her so long. I lift a foot carefully. My thighs part, and her fingertips move slow and light over the thatch that I have never bothered trimming.

She whispers into my ear: hold on. Then she disappears into the bedroom, her feet leaving little puddles on the floor.

What now? I wonder. She didn't bring anything with her. At least, I didn't think she did. But never underestimate Jill.

I think back to a long conversation we had on grass under the stars freshman year. We discussed life, sex, my devout Catholicism, her not-so-devout Catholicism. I had asked her what she really wanted in life. She had smiled and said a big house in Maui and a hot car. I had asked if she would buy me a ticket when she got there. You wouldn't like it, she had said. It was one of the best conversations of my life, the kind that you think you'll have so many of when you arrive in college. But, really, that was the only one. I'm glad I had it with Jill.

She returns, carefully stepping around the puddles she created on her way out so that she won't slip. Two opened bottles of lager are in her hands. I say, minibar beer is mad expensive so I've been told. She grins as she steps back into the tub. Hands me a bottle, says: I'm thirsty.

How long have we been in this tub I wonder? I take a sip and feel wonderfully cold beer slide down my throat. Jill pulls the shower curtain shut.

We come close again, sipping our beer and kissing and touching each other. It feels perfect. I giggle and start telling a funny story, but Jill is not in that mood. She nibbles my ear and squeezes my breast hard. My conversation dies but it is a good, easy death, a happy burial. I tip my beer up once more, draining it, then set the empty bottle on the little perch in the corner of the tub.

If all this foreplay has been Jill's carefully constructed campaign to make me hungry for her, it's working. Pulling her into a crushing embrace, I kiss her deeply. She responds. I break off and bend down to suck her nipple, hard. Moaning, Jill pulls my head into her chest and her breast balloons up around my cheeks.

The water's growing cold. I thought that wasn't supposed to happen in hotels. We are both shivering. Jill turns off the tap. We step out and Jill hands me a towel from the wire shelf above the toilet before she grabs one for herself.

I can't resist drying her off. I wonder what Brad would make of this, if only he could see it. The thought makes me giggle uncontrollably. Jill asks me what's up, and my answer's honest. She giggles, too. It's a good happy moment, the two of us laughing and looking into each other's eyes. I want to add something about how Brad would probably want to join in, but I don't. I'm skating on thin ice as it is, talking about him. Jill's never liked Brad. I don't want to cast any kind of a pall over this afternoon, our afternoon that she and I will remember for the rest of our lives. So in my mind I throw Brad into a safe, slam the heavy door shut, and spin the big locking wheel.

Jill has been rubbing her towel between my legs for so long that the skin is beginning to feel just a little raw but I don't complain. We make out.

When we finally are pretty darn dry, Jill tosses her towel onto the floor with a flourish. I follow her example. We walk over the crumpled white terry to the bedroom.

The jazz music coming out of the television strikes me as cheesy but perfect. Through the window curtain I can tell that the sun's moved. How long have we been in here? I ask Jill. She walks to check the cell phone inside her abandoned jeans. When she looks up, her face is grim. Ninety minutes to graduation. I will need half an hour at least to get home, meet my parents who have probably already arrived and are waiting for me, throw on my graduation gown, grab my mortarboard hat and hurry to the quad.

Seeing my face, Jill adds: the room is ours all night.

Can we come back after? I ask.

I can if you can. What about Brad?

What about him?

Aren't you two spending the night?

Were not sleeping together.

Jill stares, thinking I'm kidding.

We're not, I repeat. We're not sleeping together until we are married.

What about Africa?

I shrug. No sex is his idea, I say. If the Peace Corps puts us in one room, that's his problem.

Jill approaches, touches my hair. She says her mom will probably go back to her hotel after dinner. I nod and say that my parents probably will, too.

We arrange a plan. After we each do our dinners and goodbyes with our folks (and Brad, in my case), I will call Jill and we will meet back here. It might not be until after midnight but neither of us mention it because neither of us care. We're both leaving town tomorrow. This is it. We don't mention that either.

Jill's face morphs into the steely expression I know so well. I can't believe we were in the bathroom that long, she says.

Wasted time? I tease.

She rolls her eyes. I know what she's thinking. We could have been having hours of sex, instead of hours of foreplay.

I'm setting an alarm, she mutters. Frowning at her phone, she taps it. It's hilarious. Methodical, precise Jill. Setting alarms so that if we happen to get carried away in our passion, we will not miss graduation and worry our puzzled loved ones.

I've got the giggles. Probably I'm just nervous about the end of our sojourn here and the big bed with all its promise and terror, but seriously, an alarm is funny. I start tickling Jill.

Stop, she says, turning away, still tapping at her phone. I know her weak spot: under her armpits. I grab and she shrieks, trying to writhe away.

I love these moments. Tickling Jill is the only time when I ever see her poise crumble. She becomes helpless, laughing and sobbing, screaming obscenities at me and trying to escape. I think of all the tickle fights we've had over the years. She really could've gotten away she wanted to, but usually she didn't. Sometimes it would go on forever, me on top of her, tickling away and her almost crying as she begged me to stop. I don't happen to be ticklish, myself, so she had nothing to fight back with. And now, as we spin around the room naked, I realize that maybe all this time she never wanted to.

We crash onto the bed. My head hits her phone, hard. Your fault, she shouts in triumph. She checks the phone one more time before tossing it to the nightstand. We make out, wriggling up toward the pillows.

Jill yanks the thin comforter, exposing white linen underneath. I move around awkwardly, balancing on knees and hands, as she pulls the cover out from under me. The cool sheets feel lovely. My body's still damp and I see little dark patches here and there where the sheets absorb the moisture.

After hopping off the bed to pull the covers off all the way, Jill nearly jumps on top of me. Whoa, I say, letting her wedge her knee between my thighs as she sucks my boobs. Getting a little forward there, aren't you? She ignores me. Good. I close my eyes. The hum I felt when we were in the shower returns. The vibrations are inside of me but somehow they are going through me, like some science fiction radio signal that tunes your body higher and higher until you lose your mind.

Jill nestles at my side and she initiates a slow, steady, tantalizing make-out. Her calf slides up and down over my warm wet bush. It feels SO GOOD. I know everybody says that, but by God, when you feel it for yourself it is a huge freakin' deal. Part of me considers that it's just as well Jill and I never did this freshman year, because I never would have let her out of bed.

My thought jumps from that place over to another place, like a propeller plane island-hopping. I replay in my mind The Offer, something I have replayed many times.

Jill and I are walking back from a movie in town. It's early enough in our relationship that we still don't know everything about each other. The freshman dorm is in sight.

She stops suddenly.

What? I say.

You want to sleep together? she asks.

I blink.

She stares at me, calm. Her eyes say that this is a perfectly reasonable proposition.

I finally beg off with stuttered words. We are roommates, uh, and besides, I'm not sure I'm into girls, and, uh…

She nods. Well, the offer stands, she says. She begins walking again and I follow. She changes the subject.

The weirdest thing about it was that things never got weird between us. She offered, I declined. Over. I was the one who started joking about The Offer. Then over the years she would keep saying: The Offer stands. And I would look at her and roll my eyes.

And now, finally, the starfish got her clam. Jill's face kisses down my stomach. I squeeze her hand hard, looking away.

Her nose buries itself in my pubic hair. All I can think is, I never used any soap in that…shower…

She takes her time, separating my labia with her fingers and licking the folds high and low, high and low. My eyes close. I wonder if from now on ever time in my life when I hear jazz, I will think of this. I try to lift my knee and spread wider, but Jill's crouched over my leg. She feels my movement and somehow settles gracefully between my thighs while never pausing her ministrations high and low…high and low…

I hear a long, soft sigh. How can Jill make such a sound while she's down there, I wonder. Then I realize the sigh came from me. I squeeze Jill's hand; she squeezes back.

I feel transported, in the way that someone on Star Trek might feel transported. I like sci-fi. Jill has always kidded me about my Star Trek thing. I want to tell her now about my transported feeling but my friend is occupied and seems somewhere else right now. I feel her really getting into it. She eats me the way a cat that was weaned too early sometimes sucks: eyes closed, hypnotized, not thinking or feeling anything but the sucking.

Something shifts inside of me, ba-thump, and I feel my vibrations begin to swell up like a wave. But Jill senses it too and eases off until my ocean has passed from storm to whitecaps. Then she starts in earnest once more, sliding her lips over my mons as she eats, massaging my breast with her free hand. This happens a second, then a third time. She plays my body, a master conductor, building my nascent orgasm from the foundation, orchestrating ever-more power behind it. I have read about lovers playing each other's body like an instrument in the trashy romances I secretly read. Up until now, I had thought it was just purple prose.

Jill is building my vibrations again, and this time she slides two fingers in and out of my vulva as she sucks my aching clitoris. I know this time she's going all the way. The idea excites me in a manner that transcends simple sex. It's a sharing of something, it means something, in a way that only her and I will ever understand.

I've had orgasms before, all d.i.y. of course. But this one lifts me up (TRANSPORTS me) in every way: in spirit, and mind, and flesh. I rise off the mattress. My scream hurts my own ears. I hope we don't have neighbors.

Now Jill is above me, kissing my trembling lips. I whisper that I can't feel my legs. My eyes are still closed but I know she's grinning. She snuggles in tight, caressing my shaky body.

After I have more or less returned to planet Earth, I stare at Jill as she kisses me softly: kiss, kiss, kiss. Her eyes are open and I see little flecks of gold in her blue irises that I never have seen before. I run my fingers through her blonde hair. It curls naturally at the bottom under her ears, a little bob that makes her locks bounce jauntily whenever she trots or runs. It feels softer than I thought it would. I know my own hair is a little rough, prone to snags. If I don't comb out my curls every morning there's hell to pay.

What are you thinking about, she asks. I realize I have been running my fingers through her hair and staring in her eyes forever. I want to tell her I love her, that I fell for her the moment we met. That she is the only person I will ever feel this way about. That I would consign my soul to eternal damnation happily if she would only love me back, love me and only me for the rest of her life.

But I know now what I have always known: Jill will never take anyone into her heart.

One night long ago, when we were both very drunk and I had not yet met Brad, I asked her what kind of girl she saw herself ending up with. She hemmed and hawed. Maybe this kind, maybe that kind. Ha ha, I slurred, trick question: you're never going to be with anybody because you love your freedom more than love itself. She had stared at me for a long time and then shook her head. You know me too well, she had said.

I know her too well.

Maybe if I gave her the speech, the speech that I have been preparing for so long, she would say yes.

I love you, Jill. I don't want to be with Brad, or anybody else. I want to be with you. And I know by telling you this I'm risking our friendship, and the thought of our friendship changing or God forbid you not wanting to talk to me anymore, that thought scares me more than I can describe. But if you will just let me love you, and stop your one-night stands, and give me all the love that I know is locked deep inside you—Jill, then ask me for anything because I will give you everything and I will never leave you.

I don't give her the speech. I smile and make a wisecrack. She laughs.

My body turns. I push Jill down onto her back. My, aren't we presumptuous, she says. I don't answer. I kiss and lick her boobs, loving their clean taste. Jill squirms; she had mentioned once that her nipples were extremely sensitive, and now I know it's true.

Sighing, I shift my body down, lifting her knee so that I can get in. You don't have to, I hear her whisper. Feigning deafness, I settle in and wrap my arms around her upper legs. Such beautiful skin. Creamy and perfectly soft on the inside of her thighs, just like I knew it would be. I can't resist sucking big mouthfuls of it. No hickeys, she says shakily. I'm wearing a short skirt to work on

Monday. I ignore her and suck especially hard, ripping my lips from the inside of her thigh with a violent slurp. Her head falls back and she moans.

Time is drawing short. I want this to be long and beautiful but the alarm is in the back of my mind and who knows if a post-graduation recap tonight will even happen. Closing my eyes, I lower my face to her Venus and feel her stubbly mound slide over my lips.

Wowweeee, she murmurs.

My mouth opens and my tongue snakes down, over, and then inside like a curious animal. I find her clitoris immediately, swollen and thrusting up like an angry pea. It's so good, better even than I have imagined.

Ellie, she gasps. Her hand touches my head tenderly. She almost asks if I've ever done this before; I can feel the words on her lips. But she doesn't. Because this means something and she doesn't want to make jokes. Neither do I.

I begin moaning as I eat her. I have nothing left to hide. I let it all out, the hunger, the ecstasy, everything. I can't play Jill's body like she played mine, I don't have the skill. But what I lack in technique I make up in enthusiasm.

Ellie, she says despite herself. I can't believe we waited this long.

Then she moans, a long, drawn-out sound of a dying girl. A tremor shudders her. I break off and nuzzle her thighs to brush off my tears so she won't see.

Tug, tug: she's pulling me up. I rise, still between her legs in the missionary position. Over her, my eyes stare into hers. After a long moment, she opens her mouth…

Braaaaak-braaaaak-braaaaak. The alarm.

The moment passes and Jill gives me her old grin. Showtime, she says. A playful hand slaps my butt. Let's go!

I try not to fall down as my shaky legs step into my jeans. Later tonight when we return, if we return, I will give her the speech. I will risk everything. Though I'm already pretty sure how it will end, I am willing to gamble. Because I cannot spend the rest of my life wondering what if.

But I will know the moment I see it in her eyes. If I lose my friend, my oxygen, at least I have a private hotel room here away from my family and my fiancée and my friends where I can cry. I will wait after Jill has gone. My tears will belong only to me.

The End

Thanks for reading! If you have time, please review *Starfish*. I read every review, and I appreciate honest feedback!

If you enjoyed this book, you may also enjoy

The Beard

By Anne Eton

When tall, pretty Kelly interviews at Washington D.C.'s premier LGBT-centric lobbying firm, she claims she has a girlfriend. Nothing could be further from the truth; she's never even kissed a girl. Kelly's hired. However, a suspicious co-worker keeps inquiring about her girlfriend. To keep her lies straight, Kelly bases her fictional partner on Anna, an aggressive, gorgeous lesbian friend of a friend. But when the firm's annual Christmas party looms, Kelly's forced to produce her mysterious girlfriend. The real Anna agrees to be Kelly's "beard"—her fake date. But at the party, alcohol flows… and Anna's all over Kelly. Kelly pretends to her office mates that her "girlfriend's" advances are perfectly normal—even as she feels her resistance to the beautiful woman melting away.

The Beard is a comedy with sexy scenes and some explicit passages.

Excerpt follows!

The Beard

Excerpt:

Kelly stumbled, tipsy. Anna guided her with a sure hand to the office supply room, opening the door and escorting her inside.

"Hey! Office supplies," Kelly said with false cheer. She looked around nervously. "You need some gel pens? Ha, ha!"

Anna smirked. She shut the door behind them and pressed the doorknob's button, locking it.

"Or paper clips, or toner," Kelly babbled, casually backing away. "It's a regular Staples in here!"

"Yes," Anna replied. The blonde gave Anna a sexy look and flipped a wall switch. The room went dark.

"I think we should talk about expectations," Kelly said in the pitch black, as if discussing the price of a car. "I admit, I did sort of use you for my own ends…"

"Yes."

Kelly felt Anna's hands. The tall girl backed away; she came up against waist-high pallets of paper boxes.

"You see," Kelly gasped, "I know we're supposed to be pretending that you're my girlfriend—"

"Yes… yes…" Anna murmured. She began slipping Kelly's dress up as the taller girl moved awkwardly against the immovable cartons.

Also by Anne Eton

ABOUT THE AUTHOR

I write first-time F/F erotic romance. I love what I do!

If you would like to know when I publish new books, please join my New Release Mailing List, at my site! I don't share my readers' email with anyone, for any reason.

www.anneeton.com

Thanks for reading!

Anne